KIMBO'S
MARBLE

AMY HERRICK

KIMBO'S MARBLE

paintings by
EDWARD S.GAZSI

A LAURA GERINGER BOOK
An Imprint of HarperCollins Publishers

Kimbo's Marble
Text copyright © 1993 by Amy Herrick
Illustrations copyright © 1993 by Edward S. Gazsi
Printed in the U.S.A. All rights reserved.
Typography by Christine Hoffman
1 2 3 4 5 6 7 8 9 10
❖
First Edition

Library of Congress Cataloging-in-Publication Data
Herrick, Amy.
  Kimbo's marble / by Amy Herrick ; illustrated by Edward S. Gazsi.
     p.   cm.
  "A Laura Geringer book."
  Summary: When her brother Willy is stolen by the troll Grimpoke, Princess Kimbo
follows them across the Tiger Bridge on a daring rescue mission.
  ISBN 0-06-020373-0. — ISBN 0-06-020374-9 (lib. bdg.)
  [1. Fairy tales.   2. Trolls—Fiction.   3. Brothers and sisters—Fiction.]   I. Gazsi,
Edward S., ill.   II. Title.
PZ8.H44Ki   1993   91-18988
[E]—dc20   CIP
                                                                                    AC

To Charlie, Mark, and Kim
——A.H.

*To my wife Mariella. She is my gift from God and
my closest friend. Her consistent encouragement,
pointed suggestions, and constant prayers have
lovingly strengthened me and my craft.*
——E.S.G.

OT LONG AGO, in a nearby kingdom, a little princess named Kimbo was born. She wasn't very old when Spinder, the long-nosed lady who ran the post office, came to pay a call. Spinder rode right up to the castle and jumped off her bicycle. Without bothering to knock, she walked through the front doors and over to Kimbo's cradle.

"Here is a present for you, Princess," she said, and handed her a bright-blue marble. Inside this marble were all the stars in the sky. Kimbo, being a baby, didn't look at it closely, but she liked the shine of it. She grabbed it in her little fist, and before anyone could stop her, she popped it into her mouth and swallowed it.

Kimbo grew into a beautiful princess with eyes as black and snapping as black beans. Before very long it became clear that the marble had given her the power to talk to animals. She understood every word they said, and they understood her. She spent all day long wandering through the woods.

Often, in the mornings, she would go out rambling with the sleepy brown bears. She'd bumble through the bushes with them and climb trees looking for breakfast. They'd sing in their deep growly voices, and Kimbo would sing with them:

> *"Honey, honey, honey,*
>   *is what we like to eat,*
>   *but if we can't find honey,*
>   *then blueberries are sweet."*

In the afternoons she often sat with the turtles sunning themselves on the wet, mossy rocks.

"It's hot," one turtle would say.

"Hot as a pancake!" another would yell happily.

"Well then, come on," Kimbo would say. "Let's jump in the syrup!" Then they'd all plop, one, two, three, into the cool water and roll around.

But the time that Kimbo liked the best was the evening, when the birds came swooping home, calling to one another, gliding over the spires of the warm, pink castle and down into the trees. How she wished she could fly with them, free to ride the wind as far as it would take her. But since she couldn't, she would climb a tall tree and sit in the highest branches while birds tangled their feet in her hair and told her all about the sights they had

seen as they floated through the skies.

Kimbo was very happy living like this, until one day a little baby boy was born to the king and queen. They named him Willy.

"Kimbo, you are old enough to help take care of your little brother," they said. After that, she had to stay in the garden and rock Willy's cradle.

Now she *truly* longed to fly away. Her friends the birds would call out to her as they flew by. The bears, shyly sticking their moist brown noses over the garden wall, would invite her to join them in a picnic. But there was nothing she could do. She had to stay and rock Willy.

"Pooh!" she would yell. "Pooh!" And she would rock the cradle as hard as she could to make Willy cry. But hard as she rocked it, he never did. In fact he never made a peep.

As Willy got older, the whole kingdom began to worry and wonder about him. For even though he was as cheerful as could be, and even though he had bright-blue eyes that seemed to understand everything, he still did not utter a sound. Some people said that when he was born, Spinder had given him a marble that had made him silent, but that wasn't true. She'd given him a pair of red rubber boots that squeaked loudly whenever he took a step. Since Willy couldn't make noise any other way, he wore them everywhere, squeaking as much as he could.

Kimbo thought that as Willy got older, he could keep her company in her tramps through the woods. But how could she take Willy and his squeaky boots out into the forest with her? No creature would stay long enough to talk when those boots were nearby.

So Kimbo sat in the garden with Willy and watched the birds come and go on their great adventures. Perhaps she wouldn't have minded so much if she had had someone to talk to. But though Willy often came and squeezed

her hand as if he understood just what it was like to long for something with all your heart, he never said a word.

One morning Kimbo was sitting with Willy in the sun. He was quietly folding a piece of peppermint-striped paper. Willy was very fond of making things out of paper.

"What are you making?" she asked him.

He looked at her and smiled and went on working.

"What are you making?" she repeated angrily. "Why don't you answer me?"

Now he stopped and looked at her sadly.

"Talk to me!" she yelled. She grabbed the paper and saw that he had folded it into a beautiful pink-and-white rabbit.

"Pooh!" she said. "What do you know about rabbits? Why, you don't even know how to talk. I'm sick of sitting here in this old garden with you. I wish you'd never been born."

And with that, she took the peppermint rabbit and flung it into the well.

Everything was very quiet for just a moment, and then the well began to rumble and boil and a huge wave came roaring up from it. Out of this wave stepped a lumpy, toad-shaped troll wearing a black silk coat. He swooped Willy up and turned to Kimbo with a bow.

"Thanks," he hissed in a low, slippery voice like a snake's. "I always wanted a silent boy."

Then he hopped over the garden wall, taking Willy with him.

Kimbo rushed over to the wall and stood staring at it. There was nothing to be seen except two lizards poking their heads out of a crack and blinking at the sun.

"Don't like that Grimpoke fellow. Never did," said one. "He's greedy and mean. He hates noise so much, he throws rocks at the birds. That little boy isn't going to have much fun at *his* house."

Kimbo listened to this, not at all sure what she should do. "Did you see which way that troll went with my brother?" she asked them at last.

"Why, he probably went back to his castle," said one.

"Which way is his castle?" Kimbo asked.

"Over the Tiger Bridge," they said. "But don't ask us where it is, because

we've never been there." For some reason this made them both laugh so hard, they fell down to the ground and rolled under a rosebush.

"Well, I really didn't want to find him anyway," Kimbo said to herself. "Now I can spend my time exactly as I please." She gazed around at the empty garden. The great pink castle seemed to be watching her closely. She kicked a stone to one end of the garden, and then she kicked it back. She looked up at the sky.

"Of course, it might be interesting to see what tigers look like," she said to a little cloud passing by. "I've never seen a tiger. Perhaps I'll just take a look around the forest and see if I can find this bridge." She walked over to the garden wall, took a deep breath, and scrambled up and over.

She went deep into the woods, deeper than she'd ever been before. But though she searched everywhere, she couldn't find any tigers. At around noon she was walking through a great sunny meadow, full of wildflowers and weeds, full of singing birds and humming insects. Ahead of her she saw what looked like two bright eyes winking up at her from a clump of long grasses.

"Why, it's Willy!" she cried out. "I'd know those blue eyes anywhere."

But when she ran forward and parted the grass, she found not Willy but two blue morning glories trying to climb up to the sun.

"Well," she said, "those tigers must be *somewhere* nearby."

She walked on, and after a while she noticed the forest was growing darker and deeper. Soon the trees were so tall and thick, they blocked out most of the sunlight. Creeping vines, covered with thorns and poisonous-looking berries, grew over the ground and the bushes.

Kimbo came to a dark, muddy pond where two beavers were arguing in hushed voices over an old tree stump.

"Look at that stump. It would be just perfect to finish off the rest of our dam," whispered one.

"What, are you crazy?" whispered the other. "That tree stump is rotten as old Grimpoke himself."

"Grimpoke!" shouted Kimbo. "Please tell me where I can find him."

"Hush!" they ordered. "He hates noise."

"But where is he?" asked Kimbo.

"He lives over the Tiger Bridge, which is around here someplace."

"But where?" she demanded.

"We don't know," they said. Then they thwacked their big flat tails on the ground, jumped into the muddy pond, and took off like submarines.

"Well, I must be getting close." Kimbo sighed. She trudged on through the dark forest.

She came to a great oak tree. Trailing from all the branches of the tree were long shivering strands of ivy and moss, and hanging up near the top were three bats. They looked like three brown umbrellas, folded up and waiting for rain.

"Hello," Kimbo said.

They just stared at her.

"Hello," Kimbo said again. "Could you tell me where I might find Grimpoke, the troll?"

"Ick," squeaked one.

"Yuck," squeaked another, and they all stretched out their wings and flitted away into the forest.

"Oh, this is silly," Kimbo said. "I'm going home."

At that moment she looked down and saw something pink and white sticking out of a pile of leaves. "Why, it's Willy's rabbit," she exclaimed, and picked it up. "It must have fallen out of Grimpoke's pocket." She looked at it and thought of all the nice little paper things Willy always made for her. "Well, perhaps I'll look for him just a little bit longer," she thought, and trudged on.

In another hour the sun began to set and shadows began to fall. The trees seemed to be full of faces peering out at her. Two owls flew into a tree over her head and began asking each other riddles.

"What's as quiet as a snake, mean as a crocodile, and as full of pokes as a porcupine?" whispered one to the other.

"Oh, that's easy. Grimpoke, of course!"

"Whoo, whoo, whoo," they laughed softly, and flew to the next tree.

Kimbo followed them. "Excuse me, could you tell me where I might find this Grimpoke?"

"Tu-whoo! Tu-whoo! Grimpoke! Stay away from him." They flew off to the *next* tree, and Kimbo had to run to keep up with them.

"He stole my brother, the prince," she said. "So if you know where he is, tell me please."

They fluttered deeper into the forest, and again Kimbo followed them. "He lives out by the Tiger Bridge," they whispered.

"Yes, but where *is* the Tiger Bridge?" Kimbo asked.

"We haven't the faintest idea," they said, and took off into the night.

"That's it," Kimbo said. "I'm going home." But when she turned around, she realized how foolish she'd been to follow those owls. She was completely and hopelessly lost.

Though she looked in every direction, her path was nowhere to be seen. Before much longer, night fell, and she knew it would be useless to go on. She curled up under a tree and tried to fall asleep. She was just huddling deeper into the leaves when she heard a familiar squeaking.

"Willy's boots!" she said, and her heart jumped. "Hello, Willy," she yelled, but no one answered, and a moment later she realized that what she had heard was only the sound of the tree creaking in the wind.

She was cold and tired and hungry, and she held the paper rabbit close to her cheek and listened to the wind blowing through the tall trees.

After a while she fell asleep.

In the morning Kimbo was stiff and miserable and longed for a hot bath and a good breakfast, but she had to make do with dandelion stems and some little sour crab apples. She put a few of these crab apples in her pocket for lunch later and took a drink from the stream. A flock of sparrows flew overhead, and Kimbo looked at them longingly. If only she could fly. Then it would be easy to find this silly Tiger Bridge. She took another drink and stood up. Drying her mouth on her sleeve, she heard the tinkling sound of a little bicycle bell. There was Spinder, the mailwoman, whirring toward her.

"Spinder!" Kimbo cried. "What are you doing here?"

"Delivering the mail, of course," Spinder said. "What are you doing here, Princess?"

"Me? Well, I . . . I was just taking a walk," stammered Kimbo.

"Really?" said Spinder.

Kimbo found it hard to look her in the eye. "I was looking for something

I lost," she said.

Spinder got down off her bike and stood there scratching her long nose. "And what might that be?"

"Well, actually, I'm looking for a troll!" Kimbo blurted out.

Spinder squinted as if the sun were shining in her eyes. "What on earth would you want with a troll?" she asked.

"Well, I don't know," said Kimbo, "but I think he may have run off with my brother."

Spinder leaned forward and looked into Kimbo's eyes as if she were looking for something far, far away, perhaps the marble she'd given her on the day she was born. "I see," she said. "Well, we can't have that, can we? You just go over the Tiger Bridge and you'll find your troll there, dear."

"Yes, but where do I find this Tiger Bridge?" asked Kimbo impatiently.

"Why, right behind you," said Spinder, pointing.

Kimbo turned, and there, to her surprise, was a stone bridge with two ferocious-looking tigers guarding it. She was sure this bridge hadn't been there a minute ago, but when she turned back to tell Spinder this, Spinder was gone. Kimbo thought she could hear a bicycle bell tinkling far away in the woods.

Kimbo walked over to the tigers and looked at them. They had big green eyes and red ribbons around their necks. When she got near them, they bared their fangs.

"I will take the top half, for I am very fond of soft, sweet ears," said the first in a deep, velvety voice.

"And I will take the bottom half, for I love crunchy little toes," said the second.

"No, wait!" said Kimbo. "Before you rip me in half, try a little piece of me first." She pretended to give each of them a finger, but really she gave them the crab apples she had quickly hidden up her sleeves.

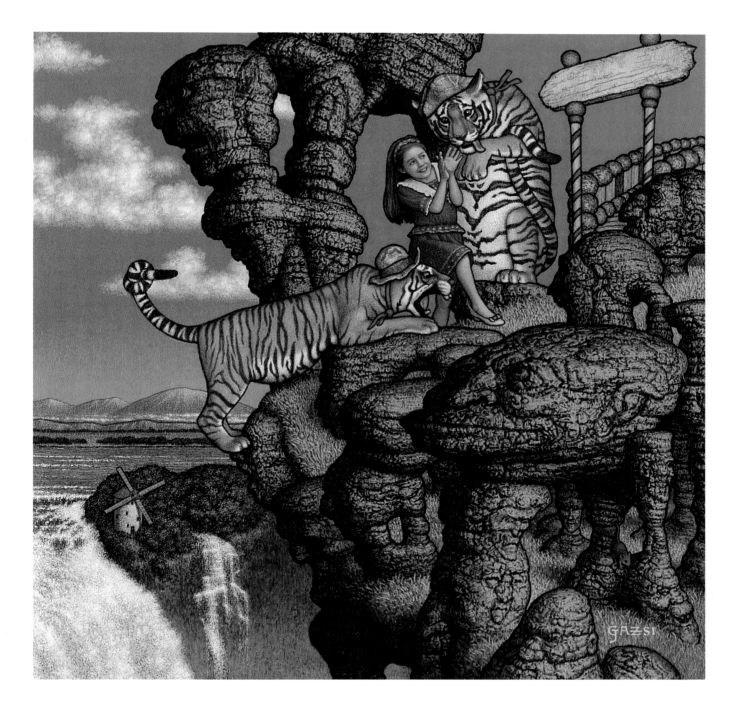

The first tiger took a bite and immediately spit it out. "Phooey!" he grumbled.

The other took a bite and spit it out too. "Disgusting," he snarled. "I wouldn't eat this little girl if you covered her with whipped cream. She's too sour. Go on, little girl, get out of here."

Quick as the wind, Kimbo ran across the bridge. But when she got to the other side, she stopped short. There in front of her was a castle made out of mud and straw and rocks. It tilted dangerously to one side, and all of its windows and doors and curtains were shut tight to keep out any sounds, although there weren't any sounds to keep out. No birds would sing and no insects would hum in such a cold and stony place.

She thought about turning around, but she knew her brother must be in there, so she walked up to the front door and raised her hand to knock. Before she could make a sound, however, the door opened and there stood Grimpoke.

"Ah," he said. "It's the little Princess who swallowed the marble. Come right in."

Kimbo did not like the way he was looking at her at all, but she followed him bravely down a long dark hallway. No footsteps could make a sound here, for the floor was padded with fat mattresses. He led her into a large drafty kitchen that smelled of onions.

"I want my brother back," she said in a trembling voice.

"Ah, your brother," he said, smiling cruelly. "Well, your brother doesn't want *you* back. You gave him away, if I remember correctly, and he's very happy here and very busy."

Kimbo wondered uneasily if this could be true. "Well, where is he?" she asked. "I'd like to see him."

"Oh, he's around here someplace," said Grimpoke.

At that moment Kimbo heard, from behind a small pantry door, a familiar squeaking sound. "Willy!" she cried, and rushed over and turned the knob.

"Drat those infernal boots," said Grimpoke.

There sat poor Willy, weeping and chopping, in the middle of a huge mountain of onions. It looked like Grimpoke had been making him chop onions all day and all night.

"He's perfectly happy," Grimpoke said. "He's only crying because of the onions. He wants nothing to do with you."

But at that moment Willy looked up and saw her. Through his tears he smiled a smile like the sun rising up in the morning. All of the meanness she had ever felt toward him melted away, and she knew how much she had missed him.

She started toward him, to kiss him and catch him in her arms, but

Grimpoke reached out and grabbed her. She stared at him, terrified.

"You have something I want," he said. "I want that marble." Before she could say a word, he began to tickle and pinch her.

"Oh, no! Stop, please stop!" yelled Kimbo.

"Quiet!" ordered Grimpoke, and he pinched and tickled her harder.

She didn't know whether to laugh or cry.

"Stop, hee, hee, hee! Stop!" she shouted, and at that moment she laughed so hard, out popped the marble Spinder had given her when she was a baby.

"My marble!" she cried. It flew through the air, sparkling and glittering like a million tiny stars, and landed in Willy's lap with the onions. Willy picked it up very gently and looked at Kimbo.

She hesitated for just a moment. Then she nodded.

An angry hissing came from Grimpoke.

"It's mine!" he screamed, and he sprang across the room toward Willy.

But Willy was too fast for him. He held the marble up to the light so they could all see the twinkling stars. Then he popped it into his mouth and swallowed it.

Willy frowned and touched his heart like something was tickling him there. Grimpoke turned pale.

"Hey," said Willy in a low, rough voice. "Hey, hey, hey. I can talk." He looked around in amazement. "I'm talking. Talking!" He threw his onions in the air and jumped up on the table. "Listen!" he shouted. "Listen to me!"

Willy hopped up and down on one foot, yelling, while Grimpoke made a hideous face and stuck his fingers in his ears.

Suddenly Willy stopped and put his hand to his throat again. "Wait, wait, wait," he whispered. "Something else, something else is coming!" He opened his mouth wide again, and out came a sound so exactly like a fire engine that Kimbo turned around to see where it was. But, of course, it wasn't there.

"Hear that?" Willy asked, and his eyes shone. "What a noise! Now wait a minute! I've got another." He opened his mouth wide, and out came a sound just like a rocket ship taking off for the moon. After that he made a noise like a car honking, a lion roaring, and a vacuum cleaner cleaning.

Grimpoke looked very ill. His face turned a deeper shade of green.

Willy jumped down from the table and danced around him, singing:

"I can talk, I can yell!
I can moo, I can roar!
I used to be silent
but not anymore!"

Grimpoke crouched under the table to get away from the noise, but Willy leaned down and yelled in his ear, "Listen, listen, listen! A motorboat!" Willy made a sound just like a motorboat, but Grimpoke jumped out from under the table and stuck his head in the bread box. Willy opened the box and yelled inside, "How about some thunder?"

"No," whispered Grimpoke. "No, please no."

"Boooom!" boomed Willy right in his face.

This was too much for Grimpoke. He leaped up, opened the back window, and jumped out. "Ouch!" they heard him yell as he landed on the rocks below.

"Quick," said Kimbo, "let's get out of here."

The two children ran as fast as they could down the padded hallway, out the front door. They ran across the bare, still yard and over the Tiger Bridge.

Willy told Kimbo how happy he was she had come to get him, how horrible the troll had been, how tired he was of chopping onions, how glad he was to be out under the blue sky, and how he couldn't wait to get home and surprise everyone. He was so busy talking and she was so busy listening, they forgot all about the tigers. Just as they stepped off the bridge, one of the tigers grabbed Willy and one of the tigers grabbed Kimbo.

"I will start with the top half, for I am very fond of soft, sweet ears," said the tiger who had Willy.

"And I will start with the bottom half, for I love crunchy little toes," said the one who had Kimbo.

Kimbo listened in terror. Now that she no longer had her marble, she couldn't understand a word they were saying. It sounded just like angry growling to her.

The tiger ripped off her shoe, and she felt his hot breath on her toes. At that moment she was startled to hear the sound of guns and cannons and then the noise of a locomotive train roaring their way. She looked up.

The tiger let go of her and covered his ears. "Guns!" he said fearfully.

The other tiger let go of Willy and bit his claws. "Locomotives!" he said.

"Let's get out of here," they said together, and ran off into the woods.

Kimbo watched them in surprise, but when she turned to Willy, she understood what had happened. He was smiling proudly.

"Great noises, aren't they?" he asked. "Now let's go home. Home, home, beautiful home!"

Kimbo looked around. "Do you know the way?" she asked.

He stared at her, startled. "No. Don't you?"

"I haven't the faintest idea where we are," she said. "I got here just by luck."

They looked at each other helplessly for a moment. Then Kimbo turned her face to the sky. She watched a swallow speeding by with a little green twig in its beak. "Oh, if only I could fly," she wailed. "I'd find the way home in a second."

Suddenly Willy laughed. "That's it!" he said. "That's it. You'll fly us home."

"Willy, don't joke around," Kimbo said. "We have to think. We're lost."

Willy danced on his toes. "I have a present for you," he said. "A present! You gave me your marble, your beautiful marble. Now I have something to give *you*. Something wonderful. My boots!"

Kimbo laughed. "Well, thanks, Willy. That's very nice of you, to give me

your squeaky old boots, but I think they'd be too small for me."

"No, no," he said, taking them off. "Try them on. You'll see. I couldn't speak, so I could never really use them. But now they're yours." He handed them to Kimbo, pointing to these words printed on the bottom:

> *Who wears these boots*
> *will travel with ease.*
> *Just speak your desire*
> *and fly as you please.*

She stared at Willy and then at the boots. She remembered that it was Spinder who had given him the boots. She took her own shoes off and slipped them on. They fit perfectly.

"Up," she whispered, and in an instant she was floating a few inches off the ground. "Up," she said louder, and again she lifted into the air. She was just over Willy's head. She reached down and grabbed his hand.

"Up!" she shouted. "Up over the trees!"

And up they went, slowly at first and then faster, as if they were two great birds. They flew high up toward the clouds until far off in the distance they saw what looked like a bright-pink seashell winking in the sunlight. "Why, what's a seashell doing there?" Kimbo wondered. Then she realized it was their castle.

"Home," she said joyfully.

"Home, home, beautiful home!" shouted Willy.

And home they flew, together.

$16.00

DATE			

APR 1994